CHATO'S KITCHEN

BY GARY SOTO

ILLUSTRATED BY SUSAN GUEVARA

GLOSSARY

barrio	neighborhood
de veras, hombres	It's true, guys.
fiesta	party
híjole	wow
hola	hello
mil gracias	many thanks
mira	look
muy simpático	very nice
no problema	It's not a problem.
órale	all right
¿qué no?	Right?
ratoncitos	little mice
salud	to your health

CHATO'S MENU

arroz	rice
carne asada	grilled steak
chiles rellenos	stuffed chili peppers
chorizo	sausage
enchilada	meat rolled inside a tortilla, covered with chili-flavored sauce
fajita	broiled strip steak wrapped in a tortilla
flan	caramel-coated custard
frijoles	beans
guacamole	seasoned, pureed avocado, served as a dip
quesadilla	cheese turnover, often filled with meat or beans
salsa	sauce
tamarindo	beverage made from the tamarind, a fruit
tortillas	thin, flat round cake made of cornmeal or flour

ISBN 0-590-97503-X

Text copyright © 1995 by Gary Soto.
Illustrations copyright © 1995 by Susan Guevara.
All rights reserved. Published by Scholastic Inc., 555 Broadway, New York, NY 10012, by arrangement with G.P. Putnam's Sons, a division of The Putnam & Grosset Group.

12 11 10 9 8 7 6 5 4 3 2 1   6 7 8 9/9 0 1/0

Printed in the U.S.A.   14

First Scholastic printing, September 1996

*Para Carol Lem
y Eddie Estrada
de East Los*
—G.S.

*Para Kendra Marcus.
Gracias, amiga mía.
¡Ay, qué vida!*
—S.G.

Chato, a low-riding cat with six stripes, was slinking toward a sparrow when he heard the scrape of tiny feet coming from the yard next door. Left, right, left, right. Chato's ears perked up.

His tail began to swing to the rhythm. He felt the twinge of mambo in his hips. The movement frightened the sparrow, who shot off into a tree.

"*No problema*, homeboy," Chato said to himself,
and followed his nose to the fence.

Through the narrow slats, his eyes grew big as he
spied five mice the color of gray river rock.

His whiskers vibrated with pleasure and he leaped
onto the fence for a closer view.

Yes, it was a whole family of fat, juicy mice moving into the house next door. Chato raked his tongue over his lips and meowed a deep growling meow. The mice froze with their belongings on their backs. They began to shiver like leaves in the wind. Chato was the tallest cat they had ever seen!

"Órale, neighbors," Chato purred. "Don't be scared of me. I'm a cool, low-riding cat." The mice dropped their things and scattered.

"No, *de veras, hombres*. I'm ok," Chato reassured. But the yard was empty. Another meow rumbled in his stomach, just barely suppressed.

Chato thought for a moment as he stabbed his face into his furry shoulder and chewed the daylights out of a bothersome flea. "Aha," he thought, "I'll invite them for dinner."

Chato jumped down from the fence and returned to his house. On a piece of fine paper he wrote, "Chato welcomes you to the *barrio* and invites your tasty family for a surprise dinner tonight at 6 o'clock."

Chato immediately saw his error, and changed "tasty" to "lovely." He folded the invitation into a paper airplane and tossed it over the fence.

The airplane spiraled down on a parachute of wind
and Papi mouse read it out loud.

"Should we go?" Mami mouse asked.

"Why not," Papi said. "That Chato cat seems *muy simpático*,
very nice, I'm sure."

"But isn't Chorizo coming
over tonight?" Mami mouse asked.

"*Híjole*, that's right," Papi said. A friend from the old
neighborhood was due over for dinner. They called him Chorizo,
or Sausage, because—well, that's the kind of guy he was.

After much talk, Papi wrote back: "Many thanks, *mil gracias*.
We're coming, and we'd like to bring a friend, ok?"

"Oh sure!" Chato shouted over the fence. "A friend of a friend is a friend, *¿qué no?*" He couldn't believe his luck. Instead of just five mice there would be six. Chato pranced off to the kitchen to rattle his pots and pans.

Whistling "La Bamba" he took out beans for *frijoles*. "Perfect for mice." Then ripe avocados for *guacamole*. "Veeery nice." And he checked for some *arroz*, because "Of course we need rice."

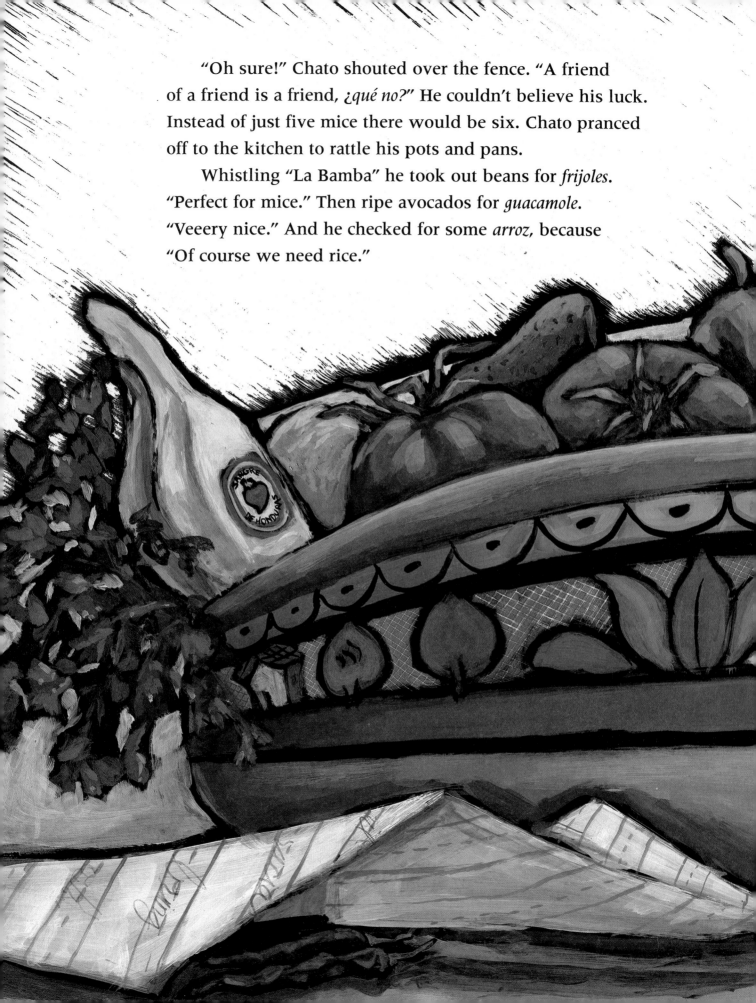

As he was piling ingredients on the table, the doorbell rang. It was Chato's best friend, Novio Boy, a cat with soft green eyes, sleek fur, and the loveliest growl in the *barrio*. Novio Boy also wore the flashiest cat collar—a leather one with real gems that sparkled at night when cars passed in the street.

"Yo! Cool Cat of East Los, Homes!" he purred. "Whatcha doin'?"

"I'm having mice for dinner. Served with the works. Help me with *las tortillas*."

The guys got to work. While Chato rolled out the *tortillas*
with a rolling pin, Novio Boy placed them on the hot griddle,
careful not to burn his paws. He flipped them over when one
side was baked, until both sides were purrrfect.

All afternoon they worked away in the kitchen. They cooked the beans and made *salsa*—not too spicy for the guests—and a large pitcher of *tamarindo*. They made *fajitas, enchiladas, carne asada, chiles rellenos*, and finally, a sweet, smooth *flan*.

While the cats were busy in Chato's kitchen, the mice were settling into their new home. They had set up a bottle cap for a bathtub, a chip of glass for a mirror, and their matchbox beds, all in a line.

But they still remembered, as the sun began to drop behind the trees, that they should take a dish to Chato's house. What did they make? *Quesadillas,* of course, featuring their favorite ingredient—cheese!

Soon Chorizo arrived, and
the mice danced in the shadow
of their long, skinny, low-riding
friend. They told him about the
party at Chato's house.

"Ok, *ratoncitos*, little mice—it's
time to go to the *fiesta*!"

So they climbed onto Chorizo's
back where they clung to his short
fur. As if in a limousine they cruised
out of their jungly yard and around
the picket fence to Chato's place.

Chato and Novio Boy were in the living room grooming themselves for the party. After five hours of cooking they were so hungry that each time a bird swooped past the window, their gray eyes grew narrow and their mouths watered.

When they heard a rap on the door they grinned at each other. It was like a delivery service with mice instead of pizza!

"We brought Chorizo," Mami mouse called.

Sausage! Chato and Novio Boy danced, and with clean paws they gave each other a "low four."

"We can have *chorizo con* mice." Novio Boy grinned.

But when they opened
the door, Chato and Novio Boy
were facing a *low*, road-scraping
dog, with a *barrio* of mice on its
back. "We're here!" shouted one
of the little ones.

The "cool cats" didn't say
anything. They didn't hiss or swat
the air. They ran and cowered
under the dining table.

Chorizo wagged into the house, his belly bumping over the threshold. He click-clicked on paw-nails into the kitchen, his nose picking up the smells of simmering food. He shivered the mice from his back, and they dropped like gray fruit.

"*¡Hola!*" Chorizo barked politely.

Chato and Novio Boy scampered from under the table and leaped up on the curtains, where they meowed for their lives.

"What are you doing there?" Mami mouse asked. "Don't tell me you're scared of Chorizo. *Mira*, he's a nice dog." Chorizo wagged his tail and let his tongue fall out.

Chato and Novio Boy looked at each other. They slid from the curtains and, fur raised, greeted Chorizo with a cautious meow.

Slowly everyone took their seats.

"¡*Salud!*" toasted Chorizo. "To your health!"

"*Salud*," Chato agreed forlornly. He was not going to eat any guests tonight! But still, he figured, it was a pretty good meal they'd rattled from their pots and pans. After all, it came from Chato's kitchen.